W9-AUE-474

Tangled Ever After

Rapunzel's Wedding Day

A Random House PICTUREBACK® Book
Random House 🏠 New York

randomhouse.com/kids
ISBN: 978-0-7364-2970-2
Printed in the United States of America
10 9 8 7 6 5 4 3 2 1

One beautiful morning in a distant kingdom, everyone was excited about a very special occasion. Princess Rapunzel was getting married to Flynn Rider!

As friends and family waited for Rapunzel to walk down the aisle, Max, the proud ring-bearer horse, and Pascal, the official flower chameleon, led the way. Pascal happily threw petals from his bouquet as they walked.

At the altar, Rapunzel and Flynn were as joyful as could be.
As the ceremony began, it seemed to be the perfect wedding.

Suddenly, a flower petal fell on Max's nose. Max gave
a tremendous sneeze—and the wedding rings went flying!

The rings bounced out a side door, across a roof, and into the courtyard below. Max and Pascal followed close behind. The two friends had to get the rings back!

All along the kingdom's streets, vendors had set up their wares in preparation for the wedding celebration. The pair of rings bounced past a dress cart and a makeup cart.

Max was so focused on capturing the rings that he crashed right into the carts! Dresses, shoes, hats, and makeup flew everywhere. When he emerged from the mess, Max was wearing a little bit of everything!

Max snorted with surprise. Just then, he spotted a glint of
gold under one of the carts. It was one of the wedding rings!

Meanwhile, Pascal had followed the other ring as it bounced onto a floating lantern. Pascal grabbed the lantern just as it was released into the sky. After a hectic chase through the air, Pascal finally reached for the wedding ring—just as it bounced off the lantern and onto the claw of a flying dove!

Max and Pascal had to get the wedding ring back from the dove. As the bird flew higher, Max galloped over to a clothesline, stretched it back, and flung himself and his little friend high into the air.

The dove was almost within reach—and Max had gone as high
as he could. The horse plunged downward as Pascal lingered a
moment in the sky, straining to grab the ring from the dove . . .

. . . but he couldn't get it! In desperation, the chameleon
shot out his tongue.

Max was still in the air when Pascal caught up to him—holding the second wedding ring! The two friends crashed through the roof of a tar factory. Covered in tar but holding the rings, they raced back to the wedding.

At the great hall, the ceremony was nearly over. As Rapunzel
and Flynn stood at the altar, a murmur went through the crowd.
Where were the ring bearers?

Suddenly, there was a clatter of hooves. Max and Pascal burst into the hall, proudly carrying the wedding rings. The friends were a sticky mess!

Rapunzel was shocked at Max and Pascal's appearance. But she smiled when she realized they were just fine—and so were the rings!

The ceremony continued, and Rapunzel and Flynn were married at last. It was the perfect wedding day!

As they watched the happy couple, Max and Pascal breathed a sigh of relief. Then Max leaned against the cake cart and sent it rolling toward the door. . . .

The end?